The Berenstain Bears and the
BROKEN PIGGY BANK

Stan & Jan Berenstain

A GOLDEN BOOK · NEW YORK
Western Publishing Company, Inc., Racine, Wisconsin 53404

ISBN: 0-307-23176-3

Brother and Sister Bear liked to go
shopping with Mama Bear. In the
supermarket they saw things they
wanted. Brother saw a toy airplane
one day.

"I want that," he said. Mama bought
the airplane for Brother.

Sister saw a teddy bear.

"I want that," she said. Mama bought
the teddy for Sister.

"Look! Look!" said Brother. "A truck!
I want that, too!"

But Mama did not buy the truck for him.

"No, you may not have the truck."

"Why not?" asked Brother.

"Because," she said, "we cannot have all the things we want."

"Why not?" asked Sister.

"Hmm," said Mama. She had an idea.

"I will buy you one more thing. It is a thing that will teach you about money. It will teach you to save. It is a bank."

The bank looked like a little pig.
It was a piggy bank. It had a slot
in the top for money.

When Brother and Sister got money,
they put it in the slot. Sometimes they
got money as a gift.

They got pennies.

They got nickels.

They got dimes.

They got quarters.

Sometimes, they even got
dollars.

9

"Good!" said Mama. "That bank is teaching you to save."

"What are we saving *for*?" asked Sister.

"You are saving for something special," said Mama.

"Like what?" asked Brother.

"Oh, you will know when the time comes," said Mama.

Sometimes they got money
for jobs they did. They
brought in the empty trash
can.

They watered the flowers.

They pulled out the
weeds.

They put more money
in the slot.

"Good!" said Mama. "That piggy bank is teaching you to save."

"The piggy bank has a slot in the top to put money in," said Sister. "But how will we get the money out for something special?"

"Oh," said Mama, "you will know how when the time comes."

Then one day Brother and Sister
knew that the special time had come.

"That piggy bank taught us how to save,"
said Sister. "But how will we get it out?"

"There's only one way to do it," said
Brother. "With a piggy bank opener!"
He got his toy hammer and put the
bank on the floor.

Crash went the piggy bank and all the cubs' money spilled out!

Brother and Sister took the
money and ran.

"Oh, dear!" said Mama when she
saw the broken piggy bank. "I hope
Brother and Sister have not taken
their money to buy something
foolish."

Mama heard the door open. She turned
and saw Brother and Sister. They were
licking the biggest lollipops she had ever
20   seen.

"You foolish cubs!" she said. "You were going to save your money for something special." She did not see that Brother and Sister had a small box.

"That is what we did," said Sister.

23

"Lollipops may taste good, but they are *not* special," said Mama.

"That is not what's special, Mama," said Brother. "What's special is your birthday. Here is your present."

24

"But my birthday is not until…
tomorrow! Oh, dear!" said Mama. "I
am the foolish one. I forgot that
tomorrow is my birthday. Must I wait
until tomorrow to open it?"

"Open it now! Open it now," said the
cubs.

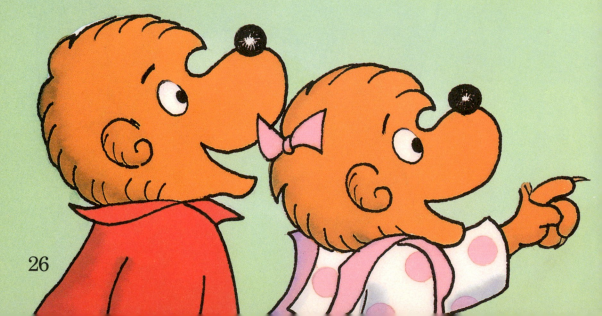

27

Mama's present was a watch.

28

"What a fine birthday present!" she said. "Thank you very much! But where did you get those lollipops?"

"We got the watch at Mr. Jones's store, and Mr. Jones gave them to us for being such nice cubs."

31

"Mr. Jones is right about that!" said Mama. She gave Brother and Sister a big hug. "I am very lucky to have such fine cubs."